Sidewalk Fun

By Eduardo Díaz
Illustrated by Janice Skivington

Copyright © 1999 Metropolitan Teaching and Learning Company.
Published by Metropolitan Teaching and Learning Company.
All rights reserved. No part of this work may be reproduced or transmitted in any form or by any means, electronic or mechanical, including photocopying and recording, or by any information storage or retrieval system without prior written permission of the Metropolitan Teaching and Learning Company unless such copying is expressly permitted under federal copyright law.
Metropolitan Teaching and Learning Company, 33 Irving Place, New York, NY 10003

ISBN 1-58120-033-1

3 4 5 6 7 8 9 CL 03 02 01

Dan said, "See Tasha and Ben.
Ben can zip down the sidewalk on his skates.
Tasha can skip very well.
I wish I could skip."

Lin said, "I can skip. But I wish I could skate as well as Ben."

Dan said, "I know what we can do! First, I will show you how to skate. I could give you some good tips."

Lin said, "Then I will show you how to skip.
I could give you some good tips."

Dan said, "Here is a big tip.
First, slide your feet.
If you can slide your feet, you can skate."

Lin said, "I know how to slide my feet. I slide one and then the other."

Dan said, "That is all there is to it.
Here, put on the skates.
Grab the gate and don't let go.
Go slow or you will slip."

Lin said, "First, I will slide my feet on the sidewalk.
Then I will let go of the gate."

Lin said, "I let go of the gate.
I did not slip.
See me skate, Dan!
I can zip down the sidewalk like Ben!"

Dan said, "I wish you would go slow, Lin!
If you don't go slow, you will slip.
Brake, Lin! Brake!"

Dan said, "You did well, Lin.
But you have to know when to brake.
Then you will not slip and go down."

Lin said, "I don't slip when I skip.
It is time to show you how to skip.
Can you hop?
If you can hop, you can skip."

Dan said, "I can hop very well. Show me how to skip."

Lin said, "Here is a big tip.
You have to hop and then glide.
You have to zip down the sidewalk."

Lin said, "I can skate just like Ben."

Dan said, "I can skip.
But I can't skip as well as Tasha!"